Digger and Daisy
Go Camping

By Judy Young ❀ Illustrated by Dana Sullivan

Look for other books in the Digger and Daisy series

 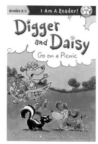  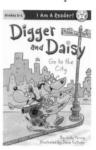

This book has a reading comprehension level of 1.8 under the ATOS® readability formula. For information about ATOS please visit www.renlearn.com. ATOS is a registered trademark of Renaissance Learning, Inc.

Lexile®, Lexile® Framework and the Lexile® logo are trademarks of MetaMetrics, Inc., and are registered in the United States and abroad. The trademarks and names of other companies and products mentioned herein are the property of their respective owners. Copyright © 2010 MetaMetrics, Inc. All rights reserved.

Sleeping Bear Press™

2395 South Huron Parkway, Suite 200
Ann Arbor, MI 48104
www.sleepingbearpress.com

Printed and bound in the United States.

10 9 8 7 6 5 4 3 2 1 (case)
10 9 8 7 6 5 4 3 2 1 (pbk)

Library of Congress Cataloging-in-Publication Data

Names: Young, Judy, 1956- author. | Sullivan, Dana, 1958- illustrator.
Title: Digger and Daisy go camping / written by Judy Young ; illustrated by Dana Sullivan.
Description: Ann Arbor, MI : Sleeping Bear Press, [2019] | Series: Digger and Daisy ; book 7 | Summary: As brother-and-sister dogs Digger and Daisy head out to the woods to camp, Digger worries about bears.
Identifiers: LCCN 2018037158| ISBN 9781534110229 (hardcover) | ISBN 9781534110236 (pbk.)
Subjects: | CYAC: Camping—Fiction. | Worry—Fiction. | Dogs—Fiction. | Brothers and sisters—Fiction.
Classification: LCC PZ7.Y8664 Df 2019 | DDC [E]—dc23
LC record available at https://lccn.loc.gov/2018037158

For Tucker, Tig, Hoss, and Valley
—Love, Grandma

To Kyle and Diesel,
who go camping every
chance they get
—Dana

It is summer.

Daisy gets her backpack.

She gets her sleeping bag too.

"Let's go camping," says Daisy.

But Digger is worried.

There might be bears.

"Don't worry," says Daisy.

"It will be fun."

Digger and Daisy walk down
the path.

There is a noise. Digger hears it.

He looks all around.

He is worried.

"I hear a bear!" says Digger.

"No," says Daisy. "Bears growl.
It is just a bird. It is singing."

"Can we sing too?" says Digger.

"Yes," says Daisy.

"It is fun to sing while you hike."

Digger and Daisy sing while
they hike.

Soon they come to a lake.

There is a noise. Digger hears it.

He looks all around.

He is worried.

"I hear a bear!" says Digger.

"No," says Daisy. "Bears growl.

It is just a fish.

It is jumping in the lake."

"Can we jump in the lake too?"

says Digger.

"Yes," says Daisy.

"It is fun to jump in a lake."

Digger and Daisy jump in
the lake.

Soon it is time to come out.

But Digger is cold.

"We will make a fire,"

says Daisy.

"It will warm us up."

Daisy looks for sticks.

Digger looks for sticks too.

There is a noise. Digger hears it.

He looks all around.

He is worried.

"I hear a bear!" says Digger.

"No," says Daisy. "Bears growl.

It is just a squirrel.

It is finding nuts."

"Can we find nuts too?"

says Digger.

"Yes," says Daisy.

"Nuts are good to eat."

Digger and Daisy find nuts.

They eat them by the fire.

They eat hot dogs too.

And marshmallows.

"It will be dark soon,"

says Daisy.

"We need to put up the tent."

Digger helps Daisy.

Digger and Daisy get
into their sleeping bags.

There is a noise. Digger hears it.

He looks all around.

He is worried.

"I hear a bear!" says Digger.

"No," says Daisy. "Bears growl.

That is just the wind.

Go to sleep, Digger."

Daisy closes her eyes.

Soon she is sound asleep.

But Digger is not.

Digger hears the wind.

I am not worried, thinks Digger.

That is not a bear.

Digger hears a fish jump.

I am not worried, thinks Digger.

That is not a bear.

Digger hears an owl hoot.

I am not worried, thinks Digger.

That is not a bear.

Digger closes
his eyes.
Soon he is
sound asleep.

Now there is another noise.

Digger does not hear it,

but Daisy does.

She opens her eyes.

It is dark.

She grabs her flashlight.